This is my book.
My name is

<u>Dylan J. Lancaster</u>

Will you please read to me?

Thank you.

MY **FAVORITE** BIBLE STORIES

As told by **Karyn Henley**
Illustrated by **Dennas Davis**

CONTENTS

Favorite Stories
from the **OLD TESTAMENT**

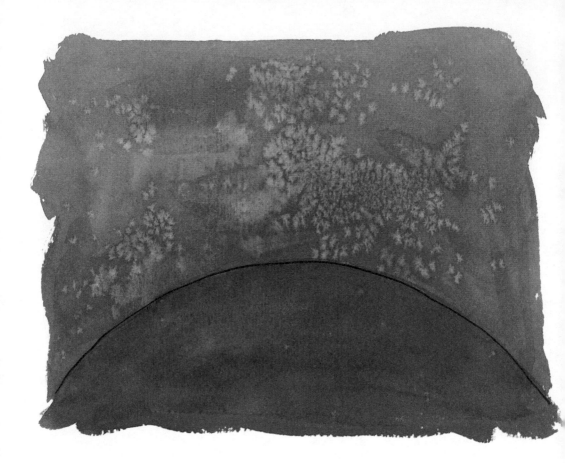

The Beginning

In the beginning, the earth was empty.
Darkness covered everything.
But God was there, and He had a plan.

Genesis 1

"Let there be light," He said.
And suddenly, golden light shone all around.
God called it "day."
He called the darkness "night."
With the light and the darkness,
the first day passed.

On the second day, God said,
"Let there be a great space."
So the space was formed, deep and high.
God called the space "sky."

God made rivers and seas on the third day.
He formed the mountains and deserts,
the islands and beaches.
He planted tall trees, swaying grasses,
and flowers of every color.

When the fourth day came,
God put lights in the sky:
the fiery sun for daytime,
the sparkling moon and dancing stars for night.

On the fifth day, God filled the water
with fishes of all shapes and sizes.
He made the birds to glide across the sky.

God made animals on the sixth day:
furry animals, scaly animals,
smooth, sleek animals.
And on that day, God made man.
When He was finished, God saw that
everything He had made was very good.
And on the seventh day He rested.

The Special Helper

Adam was the man that God made.
He had a very important job.
He gave names to all the animals.

Genesis 2

There were many wonderful animals.
But still, Adam was lonely.
God said, "It is not good
for Adam to be alone."
So God made . . .

a woman.
Adam named her Eve.
Eve was just right
to be Adam's special helper.

The First Rainbow

Many years passed after Adam and Eve
left the garden.
People began to forget about God.
They began to do bad things.
There was only one good man.
His name was Noah.

Genesis 6-9

God said, "I am sorry that I made people.
I will start all over again."
God told Noah to build a big boat
called an "ark."
God showed Noah exactly how to build it.

When the ark was finished,
God told Noah to put animals in it.
Noah obeyed God.
He put some of every kind of animal
into the ark.
Then God shut the door.

Soon rain began to fall.
The raindrops made little puddles,
then bigger puddles.
The big puddles became streams,
then rushing rivers,
then sloshing seas.

Soon the whole earth was covered with water.
The ark tossed up and down on the waves.
But Noah and his family and all the animals
were safe and dry inside the ark.

Then one day the rain stopped.
Noah opened a window in the ark.
He saw water everywhere.
He sent a dove to fly out and look for land.
But the dove came right back.
It could not find a place to rest.
The next time Noah sent the dove,
it brought back an olive leaf.
The water was going down.
The next time, the dove did not come back.
It was time to leave the ark.

The ark was resting on top of a mountain.
Noah and his family and all the animals
came out.
Noah thanked God for keeping them safe.
Then God put a dazzling rainbow in the sky.
It was God's promise that water would never
again cover the whole earth.

A Tall Tower

When the world was new,
all people spoke the same language.
They had one word that meant "hello."
They had one word for "hungry,"
and one word for "tired."
They could talk to each other and
understand each other.

One day while they were talking,
they got an idea.
They said, "Let's make some bricks
and build a tall tower.
Let's build it so tall that it reaches heaven.
Then everyone will say we are the
greatest people in the world."

But God did not want them to build
the tower.
He saw that they were selfish and proud.
So He gave each person a different language.
Now when one man spoke to another man,
all of his words sounded new and different.

The people were mixed up.
They could not understand each other.
They could not cooperate anymore.
So they stopped building their tower.
They called the unfinished tower "Babel,"
because God confused their language there.

The Dreamer

Jacob lived in the land of Canaan.
He had twelve sons.
Joseph was one of his sons.
Jacob loved Joseph
more than all his other children.

Genesis 37

One day, Jacob gave Joseph a new coat.

It was a beautiful coat.

It had many colors.

But it made Joseph's brothers jealous.

They wished they could have new coats, too.

They were angry.

Joseph also had a special dream.

He told his brothers about it.

"We were gathering grain in my dream.

My grain stood up.

Your grain bowed down to mine."

Joseph had another dream.
He said, "The sun, the moon and eleven stars
bowed down to me."
His brothers did not like his dreams.
They were jealous.

They wanted to get rid of Joseph.
So they sold him to some traders
who were traveling to far away lands.
The traders took Joseph far away to Egypt.
But God was still watching over Joseph.

A Secret Message

Joseph had a hard time in Egypt.
Even though he was good,
Joseph was put in jail.
But God was with Joseph.
The jailor liked Joseph.
He let Joseph take care of
the other prisoners.
One of the prisoners was a butler.
Before he was in jail, his job was to bring
the king of Egypt something to drink.

Genesis 39-41

One night, the butler had a dream.
He dreamed he was taking a drink to the king.
The butler told Joseph his dream.
Joseph said, "That means you will soon
be out of jail.
You will get to do your job again."

The butler did get out of jail.
Joseph asked the butler to remember him.
He wanted the butler to help him
get out of jail, too.
But the butler forgot.

One night, the king had a dream.
He dreamed that seven fat, juicy ears of corn
were growing on one stalk.
Then seven thin ears of corn grew up.
They swallowed the fat, juicy corn.

The king had another dream.
He dreamed that there were seven fat cows.
But seven thin cows gobbled them up.
The dreams made the king worry.

He asked his wise men what the dreams meant.
But they did not know.
Then the butler remembered Joseph.
He told the king about Joseph.

The king sent for Joseph.
Joseph told him, "Your dreams mean
Egypt will have seven good years.
There will be plenty of food to eat.
Then there will be seven bad years.
No food will grow."
The king could tell that Joseph was wise.
So he made Joseph a leader in Egypt.

A Surprise Visit

Joseph helped the people save their food
for seven good years.
Then when the bad years came and no food
grew, the people ate the food they had saved.
No food grew in Canaan
where Joseph's family lived.
But they heard there was food in Egypt.
So his brothers went to Egypt to get food.
They did not know they would
have to buy it from Joseph.

Genesis 42-46

The brothers bowed to Joseph.
They did not know he was their brother.
But he knew who they were.
Still, he did not tell them he was Joseph.
They asked him for food,
and he sold some to them.

The brothers went back home.
But it wasn't long until
they needed more food.
And they had to go back to Joseph.
They bowed down to him again.
This time, Joseph told them
he was their brother.

What Joseph had dreamed had really happened.
Now his brothers were afraid of him,
because they had been mean to him.
But Joseph said, "Don't be afraid.
God meant it for good."

He kissed all his brothers.
They went home and told their father
that Joseph was all right.
Then their whole family moved to Egypt
to be near Joseph.

A Basket Boat

Now Joseph grew old and died in Egypt.

Many years later, a new king began to rule.

He did not remember Joseph.

He did not like Joseph's family.

He made them do hard work.

He did not even want them to have boy babies.

The people of Joseph's family
were called Israelites.
And the Israelites were afraid
of the mean king.

Exodus 1 & 2

One Israelite woman had a baby boy.
She wanted to hide him from the king.
So she made a special basket.
It could float.
She put the baby in the basket.
Then she took the basket to the river.
She let it float on the water.

The baby's sister hid
by the river to watch.
She saw the king's daughter, the princess,
come down to the river.
The princess saw the basket.
She opened it and found the baby.
She liked the baby.
She wanted it to be her own baby.

The baby's sister went to the princess.
"Do you want someone to take care
of this baby for you?" she asked.
"Yes," said the princess.
So the sister ran and got her mother
to take care of the baby.

The baby's mother took good care of him.
She took him to the princess
when he was big enough.
The princess named the baby Moses.
Moses grew up in the palace.

God's Rules

One day, the Israelites camped
near a mountain.
God called Moses up to the mountain.
He wanted to talk to Moses.
The mountain shook.
A thick cloud covered it.
There was thunder and lightning.
God had come to the mountain in the cloud.

Exodus 19-40

Moses went up the mountain.
He talked with God.
God told Moses the rules he wanted
to give to his people.
God said, "Do not kill.
Do not steal.
Respect your father and mother."
He gave them many other rules.

God also told Moses to build
a house of worship.
The people built it just the way
God told them to.
They called the house "the tabernacle."
The cloud that led them covered
the tabernacle.
When the cloud moved, they followed it.
They took the tabernacle with them.
When the cloud stopped, the people stopped.

A Talking Donkey

God made his people strong.
Other countries were afraid of them.
The king of Moab was afraid.
He wanted to fight God's people.
But he wanted to be sure he would win.
So he talked to Balaam.
Now Balaam was a man who knew how
to bless or curse people.
When he blessed, or said good things,
good would happen.
When he cursed, or said bad things,
bad would happen.
The king of Moab said he would pay Balaam
to curse God's people.

Numbers 22-24

That night, God talked to Balaam.
He told Balaam not to curse his people.
But Balaam went to meet the king.
Now an angel stood in the road to stop him.
Balaam did not see it, but his donkey did.
The donkey walked off the road into a field.
Balaam was angry and hit the donkey.

The donkey moved close to a wall.
Balaam beat his donkey.
Then the donkey just lay down.
Balaam beat the donkey again.
Then God let the donkey talk!
"Why are you beating me?" it said.
"You have made a fool out of me,"
said Balaam.
Then Balaam saw the angel.
He bowed down.

God said, "Why did you beat your donkey?
I sent my angel to stop you.
You are not doing right."
Balaam said, "I have sinned.
Do you want me to go home?"
God said, "Go to the king.
But you must bless my people."
So Balaam met the king, but he blessed
God's people instead of cursing them.

A Wall Falls Down

God gave his people a new leader.
His name was Joshua.
He led God's people to the new land
that God had promised to give them.
The first city they came to was Jericho.
It had a big wall around it.
Joshua sent two men to Jericho
to see what it was like.

Joshua 6

The king of Jericho found out
that the men were in his city.
He wanted to catch them.
But they went to the house of a lady
named Rahab.
She hid them on her roof.
The king's men could not find them there.

Rahab's house was part of the city wall.
So when it was night, she let the two men
down through her window by a rope.
They promised that they would help her later,
since she helped them.

The city of Jericho was strong.
But God told Joshua how to take it.
He did just as God told him.
He marched his army around the city
one time each day for six days.
The next day they marched around the city
seven times.

The priests blew their trumpets.
The people shouted.
And the walls around Jericho fell down.
The two men ran back to Rahab's house.
They helped her get out of the city safely.
Then Rahab and her family lived
with God's people.

Trumpets and Torches

After God's people moved into their new land,
many enemies came to fight them.
God chose a man named Gideon
to lead his people.
God said, "You will help save my people."
Gideon set a bundle of wool on the ground.
He said, "If what you say is true, then
in the morning let the wool be wet with dew.
But let the ground be dry."
And it happened just as Gideon asked.

Judges 6 & 7

Then Gideon said, "God, don't be angry.
But if I will really save your people,
then in the morning let the wool be dry.
And let the ground be wet."
And it happened again just as Gideon asked.

So Gideon chose an army.
Thousands of men were in his army.
But God sent many of them back home.
Finally, Gideon had only 300 men left.

Then God told Gideon how to win the fight
without even fighting!
This is what he did.
Late that night, each man took a torch,
an empty clay jar and a trumpet.
They covered the torches with the jars.
They all crept to the edge of the enemy camp.

When Gideon gave the signal, all his men
blew their trumpets and smashed their jars.
This scared the enemies so much
that they ran away.
God's people won without even fighting!

Long and Strong

It was not long before enemies came again.
So God chose another man to save his people.
His name was Samson.
God had told Samson never to cut his hair.
As long as Samson obeyed God,
he was very strong.

Judges 13-16

One time Samson spent the night in Gaza.
Around the city was a big wall with a big gate.
The people of Gaza wanted to catch Samson.
But Samson left in the middle of the night.
He tore down the locked gates.
He carried them away on his shoulders.

The enemies asked a lady named Delilah
to find out how to make Samson weak.
So she asked Samson how.
He said, "Tie me with seven cords."
That night the enemies tied him
with seven cords.
But when Samson woke up,
he snapped them right off.

So Delilah kept asking Samson
why he was so strong.
Finally Samson said, "If you cut my hair
I will be weak."
That night, while he was asleep,
Delilah called a man to cut his hair.
He was not strong anymore.
The enemies took him and put him in jail.

But God still let Samson win.
It happened when the enemies
were having a party in a big house.
They took Samson with them to the party.
God gave him strength.
Samson pushed down the pillars that
held up the roof.
The roof fell in on top of all the enemies.
God had saved his people again.

Ruth

Ruth lived far away from Judah,
the land of God's people.
But she lived with Naomi,
who had come from Judah.
Ruth had married Naomi's son.
But he had died.
Naomi's husband had died, too.
Now Naomi wanted to go back to Judah.

Ruth 1-4

"Go back to your mother and father,"
Naomi told Ruth.
But Ruth said, "Please take me with you.
I will go where you go.
I will stay where you stay.
Your people will be my people.
Your God will be my God."
So Naomi took Ruth with her to Judah.

In Judah, Ruth had to work to get food
for them to eat.
She worked in the fields.
She picked up the grain
that was left over after the harvest.

The farmer of that field was named Boaz.
Boaz knew that Ruth was helping Naomi.
He told his farm helpers to leave grain
especially for Ruth.
He was glad she was picking up grain
in his field.
And Ruth knew that Boaz was a kind man.

Boaz fell in love with Ruth.
He married her.
They had a baby named Obed.
And they were happy together.

A Special Prayer

There was once a woman named Hannah.
Hannah was very sad,
because she had no children.
She wanted a baby very much.
One day she and her husband
went to worship God at the tabernacle.
Hannah prayed to God there.
She cried and said, "If you will give me
a baby, I will let him work for you
all his life."

1 Samuel 1 & 2

The priest, named Eli, saw Hannah.
He knew something was wrong.
Hannah told him what she was doing.
He said, "Go home in peace.
May God give you what you have asked him for."

Hannah did go home.
And God remembered her prayer.
He gave Hannah a baby boy.
She named him Samuel.

A Voice at Night

When Samuel was old enough, his mother
took him to live with Eli at the tabernacle.
One night after they had gone to bed,
Samuel heard a voice calling him.
Now Samuel thought it was Eli.
So he ran to Eli.
"Here I am," said Samuel.
But Eli said, "I did not call you.
Go back to bed."
Samuel went back to bed.

1 Samuel 3

Then he heard it again: "Samuel!"
Samuel got up.
He ran to Eli.
"Here I am," he said.
"I did not call you," said Eli.
"Go back to bed."

But Samuel heard it again: "Samuel!"
Samuel ran to Eli.
"Here I am," he said.
Then Eli knew that God was calling.
He said, "Go and lie down.
If you hear the voice again,
say 'Speak Lord, I am listening.'"
So Samuel lay down in his bed.

Soon God called again: "Samuel! Samuel!"
Samuel said, "Speak Lord, I am listening."
And God spoke to Samuel.
From then on, God talked to Samuel.
Samuel told God's people what God said.
Samuel was a prophet.

The First King

God's people did not have a king.
God led them by his prophet Samuel.
But the people said,
"Give us a king to lead us."
Samuel asked God about it.

1 Samuel 9-15

God said, "Give them a king.
But tell them they will be sorry.
They will have to obey their king.
He might make them do things
they do not want to do."
Samuel told the people what God said.
But still they wanted a king.

So God chose a king for them.
His name was Saul.
He was a tall man.
But he was a shy man.

When it was time for him to become king,
Saul hid.
But the people found him.
They brought him out in front of everyone.
They all shouted, "Long live the king!"

At first, Saul was a good king.
But then he stopped obeying God.
So God told Samuel
he wanted a new king for his people.

A Good Heart

God told Samuel to go to Jesse's house.
Jesse had eight sons.
God wanted one of these sons
to be the new king.
Jesse called his sons together.
Samuel looked at the first one.
"This is surely the one God has chosen,"
he thought.
But God said, "No, you are thinking about
what he looks like.
I am looking at his heart."

1 Samuel 16

So Samuel looked at Jesse's sons, one by one.
But God had not chosen any of them.
"Do you have any more sons?" Samuel asked.
"There is one more," said Jesse.
"But he is keeping the sheep."
"Tell him to come," said Samuel.

When he came, God said, "This is the one."
His name was David.
Samuel told David that one day
he would be the new king.

The Giant

The enemies of God's people came out to fight.
They sent their best fighter out first.
His name was Goliath.
He was over nine feet tall.
He called to the army of Saul,
"Choose a man to come and fight me.
If he wins, we will be your servants.
But if I win, you will be our servants!"
The men in Saul's army were afraid.
They knew Goliath was stronger than they were.
No one wanted to fight him.

Now David's brothers were in Saul's army.
But David was at home keeping the sheep.
One day, David's father called him.
"Take this bread to your brothers," he said.
So David got to go to his brothers.
He got to see the army.

He also got to see Goliath.

And he saw how everyone was afraid of him.

"I will fight Goliath," said David.

But Saul said, "You are only a boy.

How can you fight Goliath?"

"God will help me," said David.

So Saul gave David his armor and helmet.
He gave him a sword.
David tried them on.
But they were too heavy.
David gave them back to Saul.
"I am not used to these," he said.

Instead, David chose five smooth stones
from a stream.
He took his sling in his hand.
David called to Goliath, "You come
with a sword and a spear.
But I come to you in the name of God.
This battle is the Lord's."

The giant came closer to fight David.
But David put a stone in his sling.
He threw the stone at Goliath.

The stone hit Goliath right in his forehead.
And Goliath fell down.
David trusted God.
God helped David win.
All the people were glad.

King David

Saul chased David.

But he never caught him.

God was taking care of David.

After Saul died, David became the king.

David was a good king.

He loved God.

He wrote songs about his love for God.

1 Samuel 23—2 Samuel 8, & Psalms 23 & 148

David wrote, "The Lord is my shepherd.
I shall not want.
He makes me lie down in green pastures.
He leads me beside still waters."

He wrote, "Praise the Lord.
Praise him, sun and moon.
Praise him, all you shining stars.
Praise him, snow and clouds.
Praise him, mountains and trees.
Praise him, animals.
Praise him, old men and children.
Praise the Lord."

Solomon

King David had a son named Solomon.
Solomon grew up to be the king after David.
One night, God asked Solomon
"What would you like to have, Solomon?"
Solomon said, "I just want to be wise."
God said, "I will give you a wise heart."

1 Kings 1-8

So Solomon was the wisest king in the world.
Many people came to ask him questions
and hear him teach.
God also made Solomon very rich.
And God's people did not have enemies.
They all lived in peace.

Then Solomon chose workers
to build a special house.
It was a beautiful temple for God.
It was a place where the people could worship.

And when it was finished,
Solomon lifted his hands to heaven.
"Praise the Lord," he said.
"He has kept all of his promises.
May he be with us forever."

Food from Birds

After Solomon, many kings were bad.
They forgot God.
They began to worship statues
made of stone and wood.
God was very unhappy about this.

1 Kings 17

So God chose a man to remind the kings
that he was the only true God.
Elijah was the man God chose.
Elijah was a prophet.
He told the kings what God wanted them to do.

Ahab was one of those mean kings.
He would not even listen to Elijah.
He did not want to do what God wanted.
Elijah said, "Because you are a bad king,
no rain will come for a long time."

Since there was no rain,
there was not much food.
Even Elijah had no food.
But God took care of Elijah.
He showed Elijah a brook
where he could get water.
Elijah lived by the brook.

Ravens brought him bread and meat
every morning.
They brought him bread and meat
every evening.
And Elijah drank water from the brook.

A Boy King

Josiah was eight years old
when he became king.
He was a good king.
He obeyed God.
Parts of God's temple
were broken and old.
Josiah got workers
to build it back.

2 Kings 22 & 23

One day, the priest found something
in the temple.
It was something important.
It was the Book of the Law of God.
It had been forgotten for many years.

He took the book to King Josiah.
The king read it.
"We must follow these laws," he said.
"We must do what God wants."
And they did.
God was happy with King Josiah.
And God blessed him.

In the Fire

One day, the king of Babylon set up
a tall, gold statue.
He told the people,
"Horns and pipes will play.
When you hear the music, bow down.
Worship the statue.
If you don't I will throw you
into a big fire."
Shadrach, Meshach and Abednego knew
they could only worship the true God.
They heard the music.
But they did not bow down.

Daniel 3

Someone told the king.
He called Shadrach, Meshach and Abednego.
"Bow down and worship the statue," he said.
But they said,
"We will never worship a statue."

The king was very angry.
He called his servants.
"Make the fire as hot as you can.
And throw these men into it," he said.
So his helpers made a hot, hot fire.
They threw Shadrach, Meshach and Abednego
into the fire.

But the king could not believe his eyes.
Suddenly there were four men in the fire.
One looked like a son of God.
They were walking around.
They were not burning!

"Come out!" the king called.

Shadrach, Meshach, and Abednego came out.

They were not burned.

They did not even smell like smoke!

The king was amazed.

He praised God.

He knew God had saved them.

Spending the Night with Lions

God blessed Daniel.

He made Daniel very wise.

The king planned to make Daniel
ruler of all the land.

Now the other wise men were jealous.

They tried to find something bad about Daniel.

But Daniel was a good man.

He always prayed to God.

He always obeyed God.

The men could not find anything bad.

So they made a plan.

Daniel 6

They went to the king.
"Let's make a new law," they said.
"Let's say that everyone has to pray to you.
If they don't, we will throw them
into the lions' den."
That sounded good to the king.
He made it a new law.

Daniel heard about the new law.
But he went to his room and prayed anyway.
Now the men knew Daniel would pray.
They saw him and took him to the king.
"Let's throw Daniel into the lions' den,"
they said.

The king was sorry.
He liked Daniel.
But he could not change his law.
The men's plan had worked.
They threw Daniel to the lions.

The next morning, the king got up early.
He ran to the lions' den.
"Daniel, did God save you?" he called.
"Yes, king," said Daniel.
"God sent an angel to close the lions' mouths."
The king was happy.
He took Daniel out.
God had saved him.

Inside a Fish

One day God spoke to a man named Jonah.
"You must go to the city of Ninevah,"
God said.
"They are doing bad things there.
You must tell them to stop."

Jonah did not obey God.

He got on a big ship.

He tried to sail away from God.

But God knew where Jonah was.

He sent a big storm.

"Why has a storm come?" asked the sailors.

"It came because of me," said Jonah.

"If you throw me into the sea, it will stop."

So they threw Jonah into the sea.
And the storm did stop.
But a big fish swam up and swallowed Jonah.
Inside the fish, Jonah prayed and prayed.
After three days and nights, God saved him.
He made that fish spit Jonah out on the land.

Then God said, "Jonah, go to Ninevah!"
And Jonah went!
He told the people to stop being bad.
The people listened to Jonah.
And they started doing good things.
God was glad that Jonah had obeyed.

Favorite Stories
from the **NEW TESTAMENT**

The Angel's Secret

Gabriel was an angel.
He obeyed God.
Sometimes he took special news
from God to people on earth.

Luke 1

One day God sent Gabriel to a young lady.
Her name was Mary.
Gabriel went to Mary.
He said, "Greetings!
God is with you!"

Mary was afraid.

She wondered what he meant.

But Gabriel said, "Do not be afraid.

God loves you.

He is going to give you a baby.

You will name him Jesus.

He will be God's Son!"

Mary was surprised.
"How can this be true?" she asked.
"Nothing is impossible with God,"
said Gabriel.

"I believe you," said Mary.
"I will do whatever God wants."
Then Gabriel left Mary.

The Most Special Baby

Now Mary loved a man named Joseph.
They were going to get married.
One day Joseph had to take a trip
to the city of Bethlehem.
So Mary went with him.

Luke 2

The city of Bethlehem was crowded.
Many people had come there.
Joseph and Mary looked for a place to stay.
But there was no room in any house.

All the beds were full.
People were even sleeping on the floors.
So Joseph and Mary had to stay in a stable
where the donkeys and horses stayed.

That night, the baby was born.
It was God's baby son.
Mary and Joseph named him Jesus,
just as the angel had told them to do.
They wrapped him up so he would be warm.

Mary made a soft bed for him in a manger.
The baby Jesus slept there.
Mary loved him.
Joseph loved him.
And God loved him.

Good News

It was still night.
Outside the town of Bethlehem,
some sheep were sleeping.
Shepherds were watching them.
Suddenly an angel came to the shepherds.
And God's glory shone around them.
They were afraid.

Luke 2

But the angel said, "Do not be afraid.
I am bringing you good news.
This is happy news for all the people:
today in Bethlehem, God's Son was born.
You can go see him.
He is wrapped warm and snug in a manger!"

Then many, many angels came from heaven.
They praised God.
"Glory to God in the highest,
and peace on earth!"

When the angels left, the shepherds said,
"Let's go find this baby!"
So they hurried to town.
They found the stable.
And they saw the new baby.

Then the shepherds left, thanking God.
They told everyone what had happened.
The people were amazed.
And Mary always remembered this special time.

Visitors from the East

God put a special star in the sky
when Jesus was born.
Some wise men who lived in the east
saw this star.
They knew it was a sign.
It meant that a baby king had been born.
These wise men wanted to visit the baby.
So they followed the star for a long way.

Matthew 2

The wise men went to King Herod in Jerusalem.
"We know a baby king was born," they said.
"Can you tell us where he is?"
This worried the king.
He did not like anyone else
to be called the king.

He did not know this baby king
was the king of heaven and earth.
He did not know this baby king was God's Son.
"I do not know this new king,"
said King Herod.
"But go and find him.
Then tell me where he is."

So the wise men went on.
And the star led them right to the place
where Jesus was.
They were very happy they had found him.
They bowed down.
They gave him gifts: sweet-smelling gifts,
sparkling, golden gifts.

God knew King Herod did not like
anyone else to be called the king.
God sent the wise men a dream.
This dream told them not to tell King Herod
where the baby was.
So the wise men went home a different way.

The Man Who Could Not Talk

Zechariah worked in God's temple.
He loved God.
His wife Elizabeth loved God.
They were very old.
But they had no children.

Luke 1

One day at the temple,
an angel came to Zechariah.
The angel said, "I am Gabriel.
I have good news.
You and Elizabeth will have a baby.
You will call him John.
He will be filled with God's Holy Spirit.
He will be a special man."

Zechariah said, "How do I know this is true?"
"You will not be able to speak
until all of this happens," said Gabriel.
"Then you will know that this is true."

When Zechariah came out of the temple,
he could not talk.
He could only move his hands
to tell what he wanted to say.

It all happened as the angel said.
Zechariah and Elizabeth did have a baby.
Everyone wanted to name him Zechariah
like his father.
But Zechariah shook his head.
He remembered what the angel told him.
He wrote on a tablet: "His name is John."
Then God made him able to talk again.
And Zechariah praised God.

In the Jordan River

Zechariah and Elizabeth's baby John grew up.
He lived in the desert.
His clothes were made of camel's hair.
He wore a leather belt.
And he ate locusts and wild honey.
He told the people about God.
He also told them that a special man
would come soon: Jesus, the Son of God.

Luke 3

Many people listened to John.
John told them to stop doing bad
and to start doing good.

He baptized people in the Jordan River.
He dipped them quickly under the water.
This showed everyone that they
wanted to follow God.
They wanted to stop being bad.
They wanted to start being good.

One day Jesus came to the river.

Jesus asked John to baptize him.

John knew Jesus was the Son of God.

John said, "You are greater than I am.

You should baptize me."

But Jesus said, "No.

I want to do everything that is right."

So John baptized Jesus.

As soon as Jesus came up out of the water,
the Spirit of God came down from heaven.
It looked like a dove.
It landed on Jesus.
And God said, "This is my Son.
I love him.
I am pleased with him."

Helpers and Friends

Jesus knew that he had much work to do.
He wanted to have some good friends
who could help him.
One day Jesus was walking
by the Sea of Galilee.
He saw two boats there.
Peter and Andrew were fishing from one boat.
James and John were mending a net
in the other boat.
Jesus called to them, "Come and follow me."
And they did.

Luke 5 & 6

Later, Jesus passed by a tax office.
There was a man there named Matthew.
Matthew's job was to take the taxes,
the money the people paid to the king.
Jesus looked at Matthew.
"Follow me," Jesus said.
Matthew got up and followed Jesus.

Jesus asked twelve men to be his helpers.
Besides Peter, Andrew, James, John and
Matthew, he called Philip, Bartholomew,
Thomas, another man named James,
Simon, Thaddaeus and Judas.

A Wedding Party

One day, Jesus and his helper friends
went to a wedding party.
It was a happy time for everyone.
There was food to eat and wine to drink.

John 2

But Jesus' mother came over to him.
"Something terrible has happened," she said.
"They have run out of wine!"
Then she looked at the servants.
"Do whatever Jesus tells you," she said.

There were six very big stone jars nearby.
Jesus told the servants, "Fill those jars
with water."
So the servants filled the jars to the top.
"Now dip some out," said Jesus.
"Give it to the people."

The servants dipped out the water.
But it was not water anymore!
It was wine!

The people drank it.
Some of them said it was the best wine
at the party.
They did not know it had been
plain water.
But the servants knew.
God had given Jesus special power,
because Jesus was God's Son.

On a Mountain

Old men went to see Jesus.
Children went to see Jesus.
Young men and women,
mothers and fathers went to see Jesus.

Matthew 5 & 6

Happy people, sad people, well people,
sick people went to see Jesus.
They wanted to hear what Jesus said.

Jesus saw the people coming.
So he went up the side of a mountain.
He sat down.
"Look at the birds," he said.
"Do they have barns
where they keep their food?
No, God feeds them."

"And look at the flowers.
They do not work.
They do not make clothes to wear.
God dresses them in clothes
more beautiful than a king's."

"You are more important than birds.
You are more important than flowers.
So do not worry.
If God takes care of them,
he will take care of you."

The Treasure and the Pearl

"God's kingdom is like a treasure," said Jesus.

It is like a treasure hidden in a field.

A man was working in the field.

He did not know about the treasure.

Tap, tap.

His shovel bumped something.

He looked at it.

He dusted it off.

Matthew 13

It was real treasure!
He was so excited!
He quickly hid the treasure again.
Then he sold everything he had.
He took the money and bought the field.
Then he ran back and dug up the treasure.

"God's kingdom is like a man who
buys and sells," said Jesus.
This man looks for good things
people would like to buy.
He gets those things and sells them to people.
One day this man was looking for pearls.
He looked and looked.
Then he saw it!

It was a perfect, beautiful pearl!
And it cost a lot of money.
But the man did not care.
He sold everything else he had.
He took the money and bought the pearl.
God's kingdom is the real treasure.
God's kingdom is perfect like the pearl.
It is better than anything else in the world.
It is worth anything you might give up for it.

Wind and Waves

It was late in the day.
Jesus was teaching by the lake.
Many people had come to see him.
And Jesus was tired.
"Let's go to the other side
of the lake," he said to his friends.

Matthew 8, Mark 4, & Luke 8

So they got into their boat.
They started to sail across the lake.
The boat rocked gently up and down.

But the wind began to blow stronger.
The waves began to crash into the boat.
It bobbed high and then dipped low.
Water sloshed into the boat!
Everyone was afraid.
Everyone but Jesus.

Jesus was asleep on a pillow
in the back of the boat.
His friends woke him up.
"Jesus! Don't you hear the wind howling?
Can't you feel the boat tossing?
We are all going to drown!"
"Why are you afraid?" Jesus asked.

Then he looked at the wind and the stormy sea.
"Peace!" he said. "Be still."
The wind stopped blowing.
The waves stopped crashing.
Everything was quiet and still.
Jesus' friends were amazed.
"Even the wind and the waves obey Jesus,"
they said.

A Big Picnic

More than 10 people,
more than 50 people,
more than 100 people,
more than 1,000 people,
5,000 people had come to hear Jesus.
They stayed all afternoon.
At dinnertime, they were still listening
to Jesus.

Matthew 14, Mark 6, & Luke 9

Jesus' friends said, "Let's tell
these people to leave now.
They can go and get something to eat."
"They do not need to go," said Jesus.
"But we do not have the money
to buy food for them," said Philip.

"You are right," said Andrew.
"And I only know one person who brought food.
A little boy here has five loaves of bread
and two fish.
That is not enough to feed 5,000 people!"

But Jesus said, "Tell the people to sit down."
Everyone sat down on the soft grass.
Jesus took the five loaves and the two fish.
He prayed and thanked God for the food.
Then his friends began to give food
to the people.

Now, there were not only five loaves
and two fish.
There was plenty of bread and fish
for everyone.
Each person got to eat as much as he wanted.

Open Eyes

He could not see flowers.
He could not see people.
He could not see anything.
He had been blind ever since he was born.
But something special happened
to this blind man:
Jesus saw him.

Jesus did something strange.
He spit on the dirt and made some mud.
Then he put the mud on the man's eyes.
"Go and wash your eyes," Jesus said.

The man did what Jesus said.
He washed the mud off his eyes.
He looked around.
He could see!
And the man worshipped Jesus.

A Good Neighbor

"I know that I should love God,"
a man once said to Jesus.
"I should love him with all my heart.
And I should love my neighbor, too.
But who is my neighbor?"
Jesus told him this story.

Luke 10

There was a man walking along a road.
He was going on a trip.
Suddenly, robbers jumped out at him.
They hit him.
They took all the things he had with him.
And they left him, hurt, lying by the road.

A short time later, step, step, step,
someone came down the road.
It was a man who worked in God's temple.
He could help the hurt man!
But, no, when he saw the hurt man,
he crossed the road.
He passed by on the other side!
Soon another man came.
But he passed by, too.

Then, clop, clop, clip, clop,
along came a man on a donkey.
This was a man from a different country.
When he saw the hurt man, he stopped.
He put bandages on his hurt places.
And he took the man to a house
where he could rest and get well.

Jesus finished his story.

He looked at the man.

"Who was a neighbor to the hurt man?"
Jesus asked.

"The one who helped him," said the man.

"Then you can be a neighbor to anyone
who needs your help," said Jesus.

The Lost Son

"There was once a man who had two sons,"
said Jesus.
"The younger son was not happy at home.
He dreamed of an exciting life far away.
One day, he decided to leave his home.
So he went to his dad.
'I know that part of your land is mine,'
he said.
'I want you to pay me for my share.'

Luke 15

The father gave the son what he wanted.
The son took it all and went far away.
At first he was happy.
He did whatever he wanted to do.
He went wherever he wanted to go.
He bought whatever he wanted to buy.

Before long he spent all his money.

He did not even have the money to buy food.

So he got a job feeding pigs.

He was sad.

He wanted to go home.

He was also afraid.

Maybe his father would not like him anymore.

But he began the long trip home.

At least he could be a servant instead of a son.

His father saw him coming.
He ran to meet him.
He hugged and kissed him.
'Let's have a party,' he said.
'My son was lost, but now he is found!'"
God is like this father.
He is full of joy when someone decides
to obey him.

The Children

Mothers held their babies as they walked.
Boys and girls skipped and hopped
down the road.
They were happy.
They were going to see Jesus.

Matthew 19, Mark 10, Luke 18

229

But when they got to the place
where Jesus was, Jesus' friends told them
to go away.
"You cannot come to see Jesus," they said.
"He is too busy for children.
He has important things to do."

Now Jesus found out
what his friends were saying.
He was angry.
"Do not stop the children," he said.
"Let them come to me."

So they came:
little boys and little girls,
and even babies.
They came to Jesus.
And Jesus took them in his arms.

He was not too busy.
He held them.
He blessed them.
He loved them.
Children are important to Jesus.

A Small Man

Zacchaeus was a man who took tax money
from people.
Tax money was what they had to pay
to their king.
But Zacchaeus took more money
than he was supposed to.
He kept it to make himself rich.
And nobody liked him.

Luke 19

One day, Jesus was passing by his town.

Everyone went to see Jesus.

Even Zacchaeus went to see Jesus.

But Zacchaeus had a problem.

He was short.

Everyone was in his way.

He could not see.

Then Zacchaeus had an idea.

He ran ahead of all the people.

He climbed a tall tree.

He had found the perfect place to watch Jesus.

He could see all the people coming.

When Jesus got to the tree, he stopped.
He looked up at Zacchaeus.
"Zacchaeus," he said, "come down right away.
I need to stay at your house today!"

Zacchaeus scrambled down that tree.
Jesus wanted to stay with him!
He took Jesus to his house.
He told Jesus, "I want to do what is right.
I will give back the money I took
to make me rich."
Jesus was pleased.
Zacchaeus had chosen to do the right thing.

The Last Supper

Judas, one of Jesus' friends, had a bad idea.
He knew that the leaders were angry with Jesus.
He knew they wanted to catch Jesus.
Now Judas wanted money more than anything.
So he told the leaders that he would
show them where Jesus was if they would
pay him some money.
They paid him 30 pieces of silver.

Matthew 26

One night, Jesus and his friends
were eating supper together.
"One of you is planning to do something
bad to me," Jesus said.
"Who is it?" asked John.

Jesus said, "It is the one I give bread to."
Then he gave a piece of bread to Judas.
"Go on," Jesus told him.
"Do what you are planning to do."
Judas got up and left.
Only Judas and Jesus knew
what Judas' bad idea was.

Then Jesus gave thanks, and broke some bread.
He shared it with his friends.
Next he took a cup of wine and gave thanks.
He shared this with his friends, too.
"Whenever you eat the bread and drink
the wine, remember me," he said.

Then Jesus said, "I will not be
with you much longer.
I have to leave.
But do not worry.
Do not be afraid.
I will come back.
You are my friends.
Love each other as I love you."

Sadness

It was night.
Jesus took his friends to a garden.
There Jesus prayed.
And there Judas carried out his bad idea.
He led soldiers to the garden.
He showed them where Jesus was.
Jesus knew he would.
And it was all right.
Jesus went with them.

John 18 & 19

You see, it was time for Jesus to die.
God had planned it long ago.
Jesus knew it would happen
when he came to the earth.
He came to take the punishment
for all the wrong things anybody
had ever done, or ever would do.
And now it was time.
The soldiers took him to the leaders.

The leaders did not believe he was God's Son.
They said, "He must die, because
he calls himself the Son of God."
So they killed him on a cross.
It was a sad day for Jesus' friends.
But they did not know that God had planned
a wonderful surprise for them.
And they would not be sad for long!

Surprise!

After Jesus died, a rich man named Joseph
took Jesus' body.
He put it in a special cave-tomb.
He rolled a huge stone
over the opening of the cave.
The leaders sent guards to watch the cave
to make sure no one took Jesus' body.

Matthew 27 & 28

251

But early Sunday morning,
there was an earthquake.
An angel came from heaven
and rolled the stone away.
When the guards saw him,
they shook with fear and fell down.

One of Jesus' friends named Mary
came to the cave-tomb early that morning.
She saw the stone was not in front of it,
so she went in.
She saw an angel there.
"Jesus is not here," the angel said.
"He is alive!
Go tell his friends that they will get to
see him again!"

Mary was not sad anymore.

Jesus was not dead.

He was alive!

She ran back to tell the wonderful news.

At first, Jesus' friends did not believe her.

But she was right!

Jesus did come back to see them.

He really *was* alive!

Fish for Breakfast

Late one day, Peter, James and John,
and some of Jesus' other friends
were together by the Sea of Galilee.
"I'm going fishing," said Peter.
"We will go with you," said the others.

They sailed out in their boat.
They threw their net into the water.
And they waited and waited and waited.
All night they fished,
but they did not catch anything.

Early in the morning, they saw someone
standing on the shore.
He called, "Have you caught any fish?"
"No," they yelled.
"Throw your net on the other side
of the boat," the man called.
So they threw the net on the other side.

All at once, fish filled the net.
John looked at Peter.
"It's Jesus!" he said.
Peter was so excited,
he jumped into the water.
He swam to the shore.

It *was* Jesus!
He made a little campfire.
He cooked fish and bread on it.
"Come and have some breakfast," Jesus called.
They did not have to ask who he was.
They knew he was their best friend Jesus.
He was alive!

Jesus Goes Home

Jesus led his friends to a place near Bethany.
He lifted his hands up and blessed them.
"Tell other people about me," he said.
Then he went up into the sky.
A cloud hid him,
so his friends could not see him.
They stood looking up into the sky
for a long time.

Matthew 28 & Acts 1